RORY
and his
Rock Pool Adventure

THE RORY STORIES ™

Author: Andrew Wolffe   Illustrator: Tom Cole

Text and illustrations copyright © Keppel Publishing, 2001
The Rory Stories is a Trademark of Keppel Publishing
First Published 1999.
This edition published 2001.
ISBN: 0 9534949 0 X

A CIP catalogue record for this book is available from the British Library.

Printed in Singapore

Keppel Publishing Ltd.
The Grey House, Kenbridge Road,
New Galloway, DG7 3RP, Scotland.

Includes free RORY STORIES character to cut out and collect.

Rory lives by the sea in
a village called Sandy Bay. Every
day when the water seems far away,
Rory and his dog, Scruff McDuff,
go down to the beach to play in
the sand.

Most of all, Rory likes to climb on to the rocks along the shore. Every so often, he stops to search the rock pools for the tiny sea creatures that get left behind when the tide goes out. Many of the shellfish and shrimps are so small, he has to bend down and look very closely to see them swimming about.

One day at his favourite rock pool, Rory suddenly came face to face with a sea creature who certainly wasn't tiny. He was so big, in fact, there was hardly any space left for Rory and Scruff McDuff to stand on the rock.

As soon as he saw it, Rory knew it was a whale – the biggest creature that swims in the sea. Rory had never talked to something that size before, so he took a deep breath before speaking.

"I don't think you're meant to play on the beach," Rory said shaking his head. "Shouldn't you be out at sea with the other whales?"

"I'm stranded," replied the whale. "I was swimming from one end of the world to the other and I decided to take forty winks. When I woke up there was no sea left to swim in and now I'm well and truly stuck."

The whale tried to wriggle his massive body from side to side but hardly moved a muscle. "If I don't get back into the water soon, I'll never catch up with the others," he said sadly. Then he sighed the biggest sigh that Rory had ever heard.

Rory gave the problem some careful thought. After a while he spoke. "Even if we manage to free you from the rocks," Rory said, "Scruff McDuff and I aren't strong enough to pull you all the way back to the sea."

Then as Rory was thinking very hard, the whale had a really good idea of his own. "Why don't you go and get more help?" he suggested, flicking his tail backwards and forwards because he was starting to get pins and needles. So Rory and Scruff McDuff ran off back to the village.

By the time Rory and Scruff McDuff had led Mum, Dad and the other villagers to the rock pool, the whale had fallen asleep again. Rory checked to see if he was alright. "Just saving my energy," said the whale as he woke up and gave a huge yawn.

Rory and the villagers
tried their best to free the
whale from the rock pool.
Everyone pushed as hard as
they could and shoved as hard
as they could. Even Scruff
McDuff helped out but
still the whale didn't
move an inch.

Then they tried putting a rope around the whale's tail and all pulling at the same time. But the whale weighed so much that the rope just snapped like a piece of string.

Nobody knew what to do next, not even old Captain Campbell who had sailed the seven seas seven times over.

Fortunately, just as the tide was beginning to creep back in, Rory came up with a clever plan. He whispered it to the others while Scruff McDuff barked loudly so that the whale couldn't overhear.

The villagers quickly gathered round the whale to take him by surprise. As soon as Rory gave the signal, everyone started tickling the whale at the same time. Even Scruff McDuff joined in by using his very hairy tail to tickle the whale underneath his chin.

As all the villagers tickled and tickled, the whale began to giggle and squirm. He begged them to stop, but still everyone tickled and tickled and tickled some more until the whale began to jiggle about and his body was quivering from head to tail.

At last, just as everyone's hands and arms were beginning to ache and they thought they might have to give up, the whale gave the loudest laugh...

...did the best ever backwards somersault...

...and belly-flopped into
the sea with an enormous
SPLASH!

Despite being soaked, everyone cheered and waved with relief while the whale did a lap of honour to celebrate getting out of the rock pool.

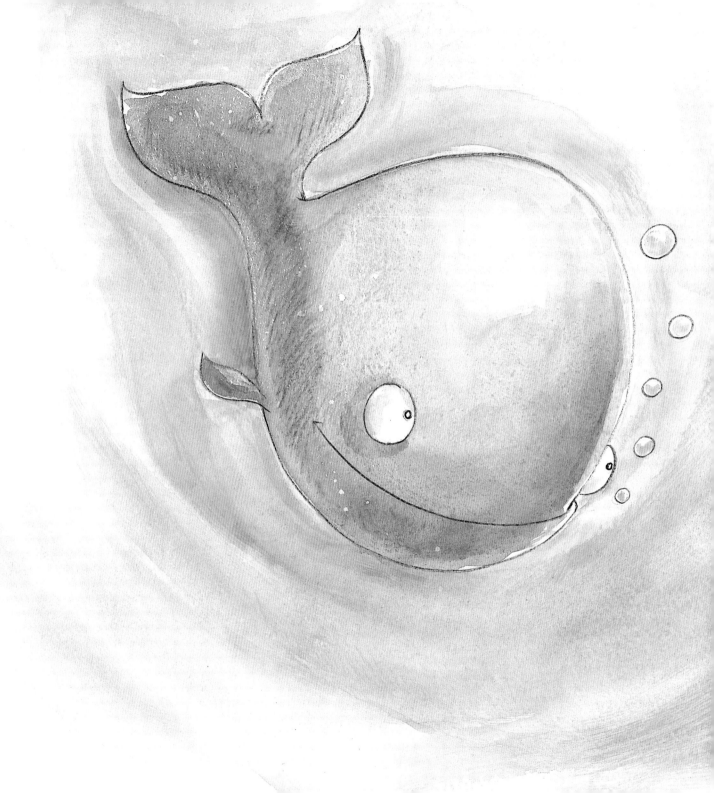

Then, waving goodbye with a final flick of his tail, he dived deep below the water and swam off as quickly as he could to catch up with the other whales.

"Well done laddies," said Captain Campbell to Rory and Scruff McDuff. "Let's hope our big friend stays awake," he laughed as everyone began to make their way home.

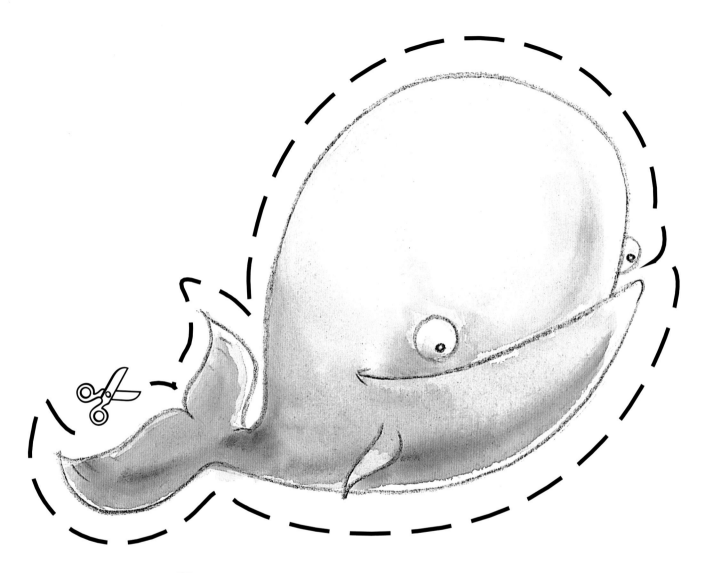

Cut out and keep Rory's whale
to add to your collection of characters from
THE RORY STORIES.